Bright

Sparks

Thank you for buying this Bright Sparks book.

We support children's reading throughout the world.
We have already donated over 400,000 books to less fortunate children.

We want to help the world to read.

This is a Bright Sparks book
This edition published in 2002
Bright Sparks, Queen Street House,
4 Queen Street, BATH BA1 1HE, UK
Copyright © Parragon 2001

Designed by Andrea Newton
Language consultant: Betty Root

Printed in Singapore
ISBN 1-84250-576-9

My Grandpa is Great

Written by Gaby Goldsack
Illustrated by Sara Walker

Bright ⭐ Sparks

My grandpa is **great**. He always has lots of time for me, even when he's busy.

I always look forward to going to stay with him for the weekend.

Grandpa is a lot like me.
He loves getting nice and dirty.

I just wish Grandma did, too!

Grandpa is a **super** gardener.
His pumpkins are the biggest I've ever seen.

Well, that was until I saw even bigger ones at the county fair. Luckily, Grandpa doesn't mind—

he's a good sport!

My grandpa is a **great** fisherman.

But he always forgets the size
of the fish that he caught.
Luckily, I'm there to remind him!

Grandpa knows all about nature. He knows the names of all the birds and flowers.

He even knows the quickest way to get away from danger! It's amazing how fast he can run.

Grandpa is a **fantastic** dancer.

I love dancing with him, but sometimes it makes me feel a bit dizzy. I don't know where he gets his energy.

Grandpa has lots of cool toys.

Sometimes he even lets me play with them!

Grandpa is very handy around the house.
I can't wait to show Grandma
what he's done to the kitchen!

My grandpa is a **wonderful** cook, too. He says that when I grow up he'll tell me the secret of making a really good pizza.

Sometimes Grandpa takes me
to watch the game.

He's the star of the team.

Grandpa tells me loads of **amazing** stories. It's hard to believe that he used to be a pirate.

I wish I could have seen his big, red pirate ship.

Sometimes, if I'm really lucky, Grandpa lets me sleep in his tent.

When he's with me, I'm never afraid.

When it's time to go home,
I wave goodbye to Grandpa.

He's probably really busy when I'm not there to help. My grandpa is so kind and funny. I love going to Grandpa's because ...

my grandpa is G-R-E-A-T!